THE TINY VISITOR

~by Oscar de Mejo~

· Pantheon Books ·

To Eddy from Los Angeles, California,
who inspired me to write this book
and to three little girls from Rochester, New York—
Margo, Sarah, and Beth

Library of Congress Cataloging in Publication Data
De Mejo, Oscar. The tiny visitor.
Summary: Gwyneth and her sister Elizabeth help find a tiny wife
for their equally tiny friend Sir Theodore.
[1. Marriage—Fiction.   2. Size and shape—Fiction]   I. Title.
PZ7.D3917Ti   [E]   81-22387
ISBN 0-394-85256-7   AACR2   ISBN 0-394-95256-1 (lib. bdg.)

$\mathscr{L}$ong, long ago there lived in Pomona, California, two sisters—Gwyneth and Elizabeth.

They were very rich because their father, Captain Homer McMillan Solo, had made a lot of money in the gold rush.

Gwyneth and Elizabeth led a simple life. Much of their time they spent reading,

playing tennis,

flying kites,

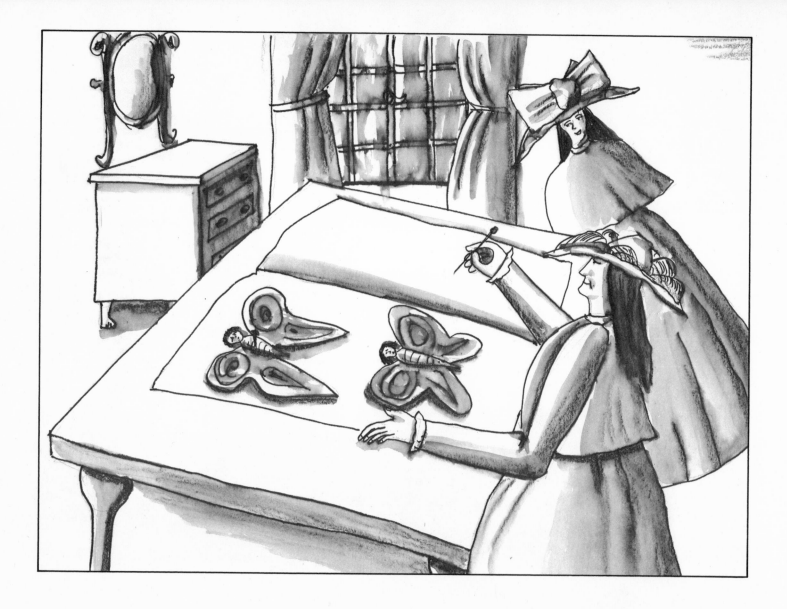

collecting butterflies,

and working the magic lantern.

Attended by their cat, Ming, they enjoyed fencing

and horse racing.

Sometimes they went hiking in the green hills of Pomona. On one of these walks they met Theophilus McGinnis.

A friendship between the sisters and the young man ensued after they saved him from a ferocious dog.

One day Theophilus proposed to Gwyneth.

He gave her a bird as an engagement present.

The next day Gwyneth showed the bird to her father. "It is growing so fast," she said, "that I wonder what it will look like in ten days."

Ten days went by. Theophilus and Gwyneth were married in the little church of St. Luke. The bird of course had to be left outside.

Next morning the bird took off, never to be seen again. As it disappeared into the clouds, the flapping of its wings raised a little tornado. People were seen flying through the air and many of the trees in Pomona were left without a single leaf.

The happy couple went to live in the ancestral home of Homer McMillan Solo.

One day Captain Solo summoned his two daughters. "Now that Gwyneth is married," he said, "we must find a husband for you, Elizabeth."

Elizabeth was beside herself. She didn't want to get married yet. Furthermore, she didn't know anyone she wanted to have for a husband.

When she played tennis with Gwyneth and Theophilus, her partner was Jim Ferguson, and he was too short.

Billy was too tall,

PIERRE LEBEAU — PHOTOGRAPHER
CHICAGO - ILL.

PHOTO SICKERT RICHMOND, VA

Max was too fat, and Aloysius was too skinny.

Her hopes were raised when her father said, "I have just the man for you. He works at the Ophir bank."

But when Horace Mayerson was introduced to her, she was disappointed. "He's bald," she said.

In April she met Robert Singer for the first time.

They became good friends after she saved him from the perils of quicksand.

He proposed to her and the wedding followed almost immediately.

Outside the church a lovely little bird was waiting. It looked strangely familiar. Robert and Elizabeth took it home with them.

They named the bird Song. It soon became part of the family.

Now there were two happy couples in Pomona—Theophilus and Gwyneth, Elizabeth and Robert. They were very rich because Captain Homer McMillan Solo had given them his fortune.

They led a happy, carefree life, playing a lot of tennis

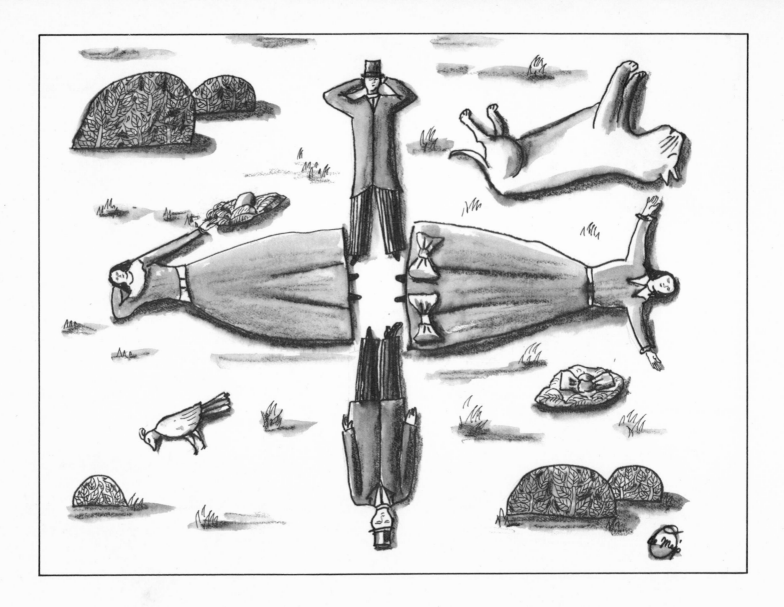

and enjoying the serene peace of the country.

Theophilus and Gwyneth were particularly fond of flying kites,

while Elizabeth and Robert preferred the subtle pleasures of swimming.

Gwyneth supervised the kitchen. She was a good cook,

but her portions were either very big

or very small.

One day she made a chocolate cake that was so huge they had to place the dining table on top of it in order to eat it.

Elizabeth sometimes helped in the kitchen. Her specialty was sumptuous ice creams.

Both Ming and Song loved good food. Ming's lunch was usually grilled liver and a glass of claret. Song ate steaks cut into tiny morsels and drank chocolate milkshakes.

The uneventful life of our friends was suddenly changed by the arrival of Sir Theodore Velasquez Cummings. It was Elizabeth who met him first.

He introduced himself to her

and invited her to see his new home, which was only five minutes' walk from the McMillan mansion.

Elizabeth presented Sir Theodore Velasquez Cummings to her family, who greatly admired his dog-horse from New Zealand. Sir Theodore became a friend and a frequent visitor to their home.

One day Elizabeth said, "Sir Theodore wants to get married. Why don't we help him find a wife?"

"Why not?" said Gwyneth. "But where on earth can we find one his size?"

The sisters had an idea. They gave a garden party in honor of Sir Theodore, to which they invited some of the smallest young ladies in Pomona.

Not a single one was small enough for Sir Theodore. Gwyneth and Elizabeth were dejected.

"Perhaps there *is* a girl the right size for Sir Theodore," said Elizabeth to her sister. "Do you remember Horace Mayerson, whom Father wanted me to marry? He has a niece who seems to be exceedingly small—he carries her in his pocket."

"Let's go see him," said Gwyneth.

They went to Ophir to see Horace Mayerson at the bank where he worked, but he didn't have the solution to their problem. His niece, who now worked at the bank too, had suddenly started to grow and was now four feet tall.

On their way home, the two sisters saw a big poster at the station. "Oh, look," said Elizabeth excitedly. "The circus is coming to town!" To raise the morale of the unhappy Sir Theodore, Gwyneth and Elizabeth decided to take him to the circus.

On the night of the gala premiere in San Bernardino, the Royal Theatre was packed. In the Presidential Box sat Theophilus, Gwyneth, Sir Theodore Velasquez Cummings, Elizabeth, and Robert.

Following an act performed by some funny-looking clowns came the equestrian number, acted with great finesse by charming Miss Renée la Belle from Paris, France.

Next was the turn of a mustachioed young man in a Mephistophelian costume, who ejected fire from his mouth and nostrils.

Then they saw the suspenseful act of a daring young man by the name of John Rigby, who stuck his head several times in a lioness's mouth.

Then they watched the heroic performance of Mustafa Ali, who held a fifty-ton elephant on his body for fifteen consecutive minutes.

The climax of the circus, at least for our friends, came when the ringmaster introduced the tiniest woman on earth—pretty Princess Melinda and her New Zealand
dog-horse.

After the show, Theophilus, Gwyneth, Elizabeth, and Robert looked all over for Sir Theodore, but he was nowhere to be found. They suspected the reason for his disappearance and returned home cheerful and expectant.

They had suspected correctly. As the performance was ending, Sir Theodore had dashed backstage and had proposed to the pretty Princess who, fortunately, wasn't married.

The wedding was performed the next day.

After the wedding a quiet family celebration followed at the McMillan mansion, and thus a new happy couple was added to the Pomona population.

Oscar de Mejo was born in Trieste, Italy, into a family of music enthusiasts. He learned to play piano by listening to the records of American jazz greats—Fats Waller, Mary Lou Williams, and Duke Ellington. And although he had obtained doctoral degrees in both law and social science, when Mr. de Mejo came to Hollywood in the late '40s his first job was as a composer. After a brief but successful career in music he turned to painting, and in 1950 had a one-man show at the Carlebach Gallery in New York City. He has painted steadily since that time—inspired by the work of folk artists and early painters of Florence and Siena, votive paintings, the work of Rousseau, and comic strips and other popular art forms. In 1955 his best-selling historical novel, *Diary of a Nun*, was published, and in 1976 his paintings illustrated the highly acclaimed *Fresh Views on the American Revolution* by Paul Foley. His work has been presented in a series of one-man shows across the U.S. and Europe, and commissioned by many private collectors, organizations, and magazines. When a young relative visited Mr. de Mejo in his home in New York City and was greatly amused by drawings of a man who resembled a bird, Mr. de Mejo decided to write a book for children—and *The Tiny Visitor* was the result.